The Lighthouse Christmas

By

MARK EMANUEL ROBINSON

This is a work of historical fiction. Any references
to historical events, real people, or real places are used
fictitiously. Other names, characters, places and events
are products of the author s imagination, and any
resemblance to actual events, places or persons, living or
dead, is entirely coincidental.

Stone Peak Press
www.stonepeakpress.com

Edited by Alicia Robinson and Andrew Robinson

Illustrations by Mark Robinson

Cover Art by Sarah Alu

Photographs used with permission from the Museum at
Portland Head, The National Archive and The Maine
Historical Society, Sarah Alu and Shutterstock.com

eBook ISBN: 978-1-7346092-2-6
Hardcover ISBN: 978-1-7346092-1-9
Softcover ISBN: 978-1-7346092-0-2
Version 10.25.20

DEDICATION

For Andy,

Your passion for lighthouses constantly drives our imaginations and desire to see new places. You taught me the lesson that life can surprise me no matter where we are. All it requires is being open to adventure and change.

I love you.

- Dad

ACKNOWLEDGMENTS

I would like to thank Jeanne Gross, Director of the Museum at Portland Head Light, who was kind enough to provide me with an engrossing explanation of the story behind the sinking of the Annie C. Maguire and some of the details regarding Portland Head Lighthouse. Without her help, it would have been far more difficult to discover many of the details surrounding this Christmas Eve tale. I should also mention that the staff of the Portland Head Lighthouse provided the thorough account of the sinking on their website (https://portlandheadlight.com). Jeanne and her team have done a great job of demonstrating that history is not only interesting but can be fun as well.

I would also like to thank the docents at the National Lighthouse Museum in Staten Island for drawing my attention to the sinking of the Annie C. Maguire. I learned about the story during a visit to the museum and even years later, it stayed with me.

In addition, the Portland Sheriff's Office was very generous with their time to help me discover more about Sheriff True's life in the late 1800s as well as how the town was organized.

Lastly, I would like to thank my family who are at the heart of everything that I do.

~CHAPTER 1~

CHRISTMAS IN ROCKPORT, MAINE

The storm outside was a steady one. Each new minute brought with it a gust of wind that would rattle the foundation of the old house and push small piles of snow from the roof. If one were to gaze out the glass windowpane, through sheets of snowfall, they might see the trees shuddering against the winter's cold.

And in the center of it all was a home. A small home with a parlor, kitchen, and two bedrooms. The parlor was the largest of all the rooms. Pine green curtains covered the windows, keeping the storm at bay. In the center of the floor, a thick rug sprawled out. Two children kneeled on it as they played with their new toys. And beyond the rug, settled against the wall, was a fireplace. The flames within crackled with appreciation as they ate up the fresh logs.

A Christmas tree stood across from the fire, as if in defiance. Although sparsely ornamented, it was a proud pine. It reminded the young siblings of the old pictures of their grandfather, standing tall and distinguished.

As they played, Grandpa watched them over the top of his newspaper. Mary, the eldest of the two, admired her doll's hair as it gleamed golden in the light of the roaring fireplace. She wished she had been gifted another such doll to keep the other company while she was away at the schoolhouse in town.

A pang of guilt struck her at the thought. Her parents had done the best they could to provide for their family. And each Christmas, they went out of their way to please her with new toys and books and clothes. Her fingers stroked the fabric of her doll's dress. It was softer than the old one had been; her mother made sure of that. The hours she had spent, picking out high quality silk and sewing it all together for her daughter would not be taken for granted.

On the rug beside her, her brother, David, played with his new toy boats and had not looked in her direction for over an hour. He was far too engrossed with the story he was telling inside his head. Every so often, he would tug on his grandfather's pantleg and ask questions when his plot stagnated. He knew the man's expertise would make his playtime fantasy more realistic, more fun. His most recent fascination was lighthouses.

"Would a lighthouse save my ships, Grandpa?" He tilted his head back to look up at his grandfather's face, though it was blocked by the day's newspaper. "It would have to, wouldn't it? Then they would be able to see the sea monster."

Mary rolled her eyes at her brother's overactive imagination. Nearly every day, her parents made her sit and listen to the boy's tales of sailors fighting krakens or finding long lost treasure. They'd said that as siblings, they needed to maintain a strong relationship. But sometimes David was just so annoying. She pouted.

The newspaper crinkled as Grandpa folded it and set it aside. "Well..." He had a mischievous glint in his eye.

But before he could answer his grandson's question, Mary interrupted. "Grandpa, I don't want to hear another David story. Tell your own!"

David shot a glare at his sister but the prospect of getting to listen to another of Grandpa's famous anecdotes excited him too much for him to stay upset.

***House in Rockport, Maine**, created by Mark Robinson from a photo taken by Yaroslav Antonov via Shutterstock*

"Do you have any Christmas stories for us?" Mary asked. She hadn't noticed her brother's brief expression of anger as her eyes were locked on her grandfather.

"What about a lighthouse Christmas story?" David said, putting heavy emphasis on the word lighthouse. "What was it like being a lighthouse keeper on Christmas? We need to know!"

Their grandfather grinned down at the children, each one now seeming to be in agreement about the story they wanted to hear. He appreciated their interest in his former career. The career of his late father. In a way, each time he told a story from his childhood, he felt like his father was still with him.

The room had gone quiet, expectant. Only the howling wind outside and the fireplace within dared to make a sound. He lost himself for a moment in the memories. Remembering how different his life had been. Remembering his father's smile and gentle chastising when he neglected his lessons. Of course, he could only be scolded if his father could catch him.

Grandpa was a heavy-set man now and his days of evading the law of his parents had long since passed him by. He tugged on his beard thoughtfully as he turned his gaze to the window and into the snowbound forest beyond. A chill seized him. The shadows between the trees had deepened considerably with the setting of the sun and the overcast sky. And the storm.

He recalled a snowstorm once that had come on so quickly that… His thoughts trailed off.

Once again, his fingers pulled at his facial hair. It made him think of why he had chosen to grow it out in the first place. His eyes flicked back to his grandchildren, noting how their small brows wrinkled with concern. They liked to grab at his beard and, when they were too rough, he would sneeze and revel in their peals of laughter. But he had a reputation with the neighbors to uphold. So, in his gruffest voice, he told any who asked that he thought it made him look more distinguished.

The warmth of the fireplace flooded back into his body. Although the snowfall outside had only grown heavier in the few minutes that had passed, he felt at peace again. He had fed four logs to the fire earlier in the evening. It was enough to last them through a story, a long one at that. The idea of which tale to tell was already brewing in his mind. The storm reminded him.

The radio in the hallway just outside the room softly played "Stairway to the Stars" by Glen Miller. He fought the sudden urge to tune into the local station to hear about the weather. Would they ever see the sun again?

"Please Grandpa?" Mary asked, breaking into his thoughts.

"Yes! Pleeeeease?" her brother chimed in.

He knew he could never say no to them. But he still made a show of hesitance. "Well…I might have a story that I haven't shared with you yet. Do you think we have enough time to tell it before you have to go to bed?"

The children didn't answer. They had already started preparing for story-time. Mary grabbed a blanket off of the back of their old sofa as David walked over to sit at his feet.

They both looked up at their grandfather, eyes wide with anticipation. He chuckled at their enthusiasm.

A rush of snow beat against the windows, as if begging to be let into the heat. The children shivered. Grandpa scooped them up into his lap and wrapped the woolen blanket around them. With a sigh of content, he leaned back and let himself be enveloped by his leather armchair as he started to recall his very best Christmas story.

"This is the story of The Lighthouse Christmas," he began.

~CHAPTER 2~

LIFE AT PORTLAND HEAD LIGHTHOUSE

My father, Joshua, had a love for the sea so deep that it was unrivaled by anyone I had ever known. He began his career as a ship's cook and worked his way up through the ranks until he was a captain of his own vessel. In those days, he spent most of his time away from his family. But when he returned from long voyages, he regaled us with the notable events of his journey.

He filled my mind and heart with the call of the ocean. I was determined to follow in his footsteps, sail around the world. It was nothing short of my destiny.

Then tragedy struck. He fell from the rigging of the *Andres* – a three-masted ship based out of Portland Harbor. The injuries were career ending. When he returned home that final time, he wasn't the same. He had lost a vital part of himself. His spirit was broken without the ocean.

He took his time to physically recover, forcing the family to rely on Mother's meager income for a while. But when he was on his feet again, he wasted no time getting back to work.

Joshua Strout, courtesy of the Museum at Portland Head

He couldn't stand to be away from the sea for another minute. So, he applied to the Lighthouse Service and was appointed to the position of head lighthouse keeper of Portland Head. That was around 1869, I believe.

I saw something of his old spirit return to him in the days after taking over Portland Head. In fact, his flame burned even brighter than before. In his days as a sailor, he had to sacrifice time with his family to traverse the waves. As a lighthouse keeper, he was allowed to have a relationship with both. He didn't have to choose one or the other and he loved it.

He always spoke fondly of being a sailor but, I knew he was happiest beside the sea with his family. He liked the methodical pace of being a lighthouse keeper: bringing oil to the lamp, cleaning the lamp, raising the weights that turned the light, keeping an eye out for passing ships.

He took any chance he could to walk around the lighthouse with my brothers and sisters and show them all the little details of his work. We would all gather around him as he demonstrated a new knot he'd learned or how to properly bait a fishing hook.

A wide grin spread across his lips any time he taught us. His stern façade would fall away for those few hours and it was those moments that made me feel closest to him.

As the years passed, I noticed how his smile became his resting expression, rather than a rarity. He had let go of any resentment that had haunted him since the accident. The weight lifted. He could let the joy of life take over again.

And it was this positive disposition that earned him the respect of the community. Most in Portland knew him by his first name and many came to the lighthouse to visit with him and enjoy my mother's lemonade.

Our most famous guest was the poet Henry W. Longfellow. He would come to the lighthouse once or twice a week and sit out on a rock on the south side of the tower. He and my father would have long chats about the changing world and the minutiae of the life of a lighthouse keeper.

It has been rumored that Mr. Longfellow took great inspiration from his visits to the lighthouse and my father's knowledge.

This 1873 portrait shows Henry Wadsworth Longfellow, premier American Poet, courtesy of the U.S. National Archives

His mastery of his duties and the respect he commanded from others made me consider him a captain of a land-locked ship. He looked nearly heroic as he stood on the balcony of the lighthouse. Like a sentry surveying the land from a tower. He belonged there. I had no doubt about that. Even our guests commented on it – his love of the sea and his ever-present captain's hat. They said the sailor's life would never leave him. And they were right. The light was as much a part of him as any of his limbs.

As a boy, I admired him a great deal, but as I grew older, I felt the beginnings of a chasm between us. He told me that I would take on the mantle of lighthouse keeper when he eventually stepped down. I had different ideas. That was the first time I had ever noticed anger in him. But I wouldn't lie. I'd rather be on a ship than watching them sail by.

After that night, he never mentioned it again and I never spoke of my dreams to him. I didn't have to. He felt it. My hesitation lingered over each conversation we had like a storm cloud. I am sure he thought he could change my mind, hammering lessons and stories into my head. After all of that, how could I not want to follow in his footsteps? He simply didn't understand my resistance. From then on, I noticed he was stricter with us.

When my brothers and I got into mischief, he would send us off to bed without dinner. Mother snuck me leftovers as soon as he had turned in for the night.

She defended me whenever she could. Her tenderness truly spoiled me. Without her, I don't think it would have been as hard as it was to decide to leave. I imagined the look on her face if I sat her down and asked to go start my life. It made me feel too guilty to even try.

There was something special about her. Even with eleven children, she still found the time and energy to help with the lighthouse. When she was hard at work with my father, I would often see her running to the house to check on something baking in the oven or helping one of my siblings with their lessons.

If my father was the captain of the lighthouse, she was the admiral who kept the whole family running smoothly. She had the disposition of a lake on a windless day, still and glassy in her calmness. I rarely saw a problem that would rattle her. At the first sign of trouble, she would simply set her lips in a smile and find the perfect solution.

"Life rarely presents you with a challenge you cannot handle," she would often remind me. It was her favorite saying.

In 1877, Mother passed on her title to me. I was 18 when I became the Assistant Lighthouse Keeper in her stead. The honor was so great, I once lamented to her that I could never surpass her skill and devotion. I was too restless. I couldn't stay forever.

She smiled sadly. "Did you forget what I said about challenges already?"

I always believed that she wanted me to take over the position so that I wouldn't leave them. And it worked for a time. As I watched my elder siblings grow and fly from the nest, I felt bound by duty to stay. I couldn't disappoint her.

Yet, at the same time, I felt trapped. I heard the stories from the sailors that visited town and I longed to accompany them on those adventures. Their tales called to me like a siren. I was defenseless. The journeys within foreign lands seemed much more exciting than the ones I had at the lighthouse. My mother called them 'far off places' in a tone that bordered on scornful.

I understood, I really did. From her perspective, she saw the life of a sailor as a dangerous one. Something that stole her husband from her and their children for months at a time. And that was before Father's injury. She refused to allow the same misfortune to befall me. So, she strived to keep me home.

Overall, the lighthouse wasn't a bad place to live, though. It sat on a bluff, surrounded on three sides by jagged rocks and an inky, tumultuous ocean. As a boy, I often pretended that our home was continuously under attack by the waves. The wind would stir the sea to violence and sent it crashing against the surrounding rocks. It left such an impression that more than one visitor had commented that, "The property is beautiful, but the neighbors are so noisy!"

Joseph Strout, *courtesy of the Museum at Portland Head*

The keeper's house felt small back then. It was just big enough for our family, with three small bedrooms, a parlor, a kitchen, a cellar and a porch where we would sit together on most nights and have dinner. There was also a small room and parlor for the assistant keeper.

Years later, it was rebuilt to accommodate two families, complete with indoor plumbing and electricity. If only we'd had all that space when there were thirteen of us living there! But I'm getting ahead of myself.

You know, my name was not always Grandpa. My parents had named me Joseph and insisted that it should not be shortened. I asked my friends to call me Joe. The childhood rebellion aside, I always thought that Joseph was an old man's name. The kind that brings to mind a weather-worn face and a grey beard. It said that I carried a pipe, stayed up too late, and babbled about ships and lighthouses endlessly.

Those were words that described my father, not me. Not at the time. Although, I now realize the irony of it all. I had tried so hard to distinguish myself from him only to end up following in his footsteps.

I grew up listening to my father sharing stories about how lighthouses could save lives and how women in big cities have fancy lace for their dresses because lighthouse keepers protect the ships that deliver their things of beauty from all over the world. He made the life of a lighthouse keeper sound very exciting. But he couldn't fool me! I knew that for every fascinating event, there were dozens more instances of monotonous chores. Hours of fixing broken things and cleaning and carrying whatever he asked me to.

Most of my days were spent helping my father bring oil to the lamp or cleaning the lighthouse. My mother told stories to my younger siblings as she juggled taking care of them, doing the washing, and cooking.

Portland Head Lighthouse, courtesy of the National Archives

My parents were happy, but I came to think it as a dull life, and I felt that I was destined to do something more important. I would see the world. I wanted to be on the ships that went by the house rather than waving to them or helping my father to make sure that all the ships that passed were 'kissed by our light.'

As I carried up the tins of oil to the lamps with my father, I became almost too familiar with every brick, every feature of the lighthouse. I had memorized how long it took to walk to the top and how many whale oil lamps we had. Sixteen, if you were curious.

I walked up those steps over a dozen times a day, either with oil or with rags to clean the lamps. It was tough work, but I liked the words of affirmation I got from my father when I was finished, the hearty pats on the back. So, I rarely complained.

Every Saturday, I was rewarded for the work by taking a wagon into town with my father. I took great pride in spending some of my hard-earned money on a piece of candy and a newspaper from the general store. And if I was really lucky, they would have oranges too. Oranges have been one of my favorite foods since I tried my first one at eight years old. I've been swearing by them ever since. We rarely got them in Maine because they needed to be shipped up from Florida.

Those Saturdays were some of my most valued memories. The only time more special was Christmas. My father once told me that the best place to be on Christmas is a lighthouse. When he'd said that no place is more peaceful or holds to the holiday tradition of giving to others more than a lighthouse, I had nodded, though I hadn't known exactly what he meant back then. But I agreed that our home was the perfect backdrop for the season.

By December of 1886, most of my ten siblings had moved out, but my two youngest brothers and one of my sisters were still living at home. They were too young for the trip into town and usually stayed at the lighthouse when I went out with my father. Because it was the day before Christmas Eve, they would be occupied with decorating the house for our special family dinner.

Each year, the youngest children would take on the responsibility of dressing up the house for the holidays. I never knew what they were going to do but they spent a lot of time planning it out. Growing up in a large family, I could always expect that someone was making special plans for all the big holidays like Christmas, Halloween and Easter.

Despite my ever-present family, the time-consuming daily chores, and our steady stream of visitors, I often felt cut off from the rest of the world. Life in a lighthouse can be a lonely one and heading into town was always a way to connect to other people and get news about what was happening in Portland.

~ CHAPTER 3~

THE DAY BEFORE CHRISTMAS EVE

A pale winter sun dawned on the Saturday before Christmas as my father and I prepared for our usual trip into town. I had just tugged on my wool coat, when Mother rested her hand on my shoulder. Father glanced at us, frowned, then walked out of the house to hitch up the wagon.

She pressed a list of holiday groceries into my palm. "You know, your father doesn't have the eye for poultry that you do!"

"You can count on me," I said with an exaggerated salute. "I will get the job done!"

The sound of her laughter followed me down the outside path, only fading when I reached the wagon. Both horses looked at me as I approached. Their hot breath misted on the frigid air between us. I patted the flank of the one nearest me then hauled myself up into the wagon beside my father.

"What was that all about?" he asked nodding back toward the house.

I shrugged and pulled my jacket tighter around me. "She asked me to pick up the food for Christmas dinner."

Wagon Ride to Portland, Maine, *created by Mark Robinson*

He made no move to respond. Instead, he turned his attention to the horses and urged them to start down the road. I watched the scenery pass us by. Shrub-covered plainlands studded with rocks gradually transforming into thick coniferous forests.

Nature chatted alongside us but my father and I were silent. The horses' hooves thudded against the path, their harnesses jingling in time with their steps. I listened intently. I had to distract myself from the stern man beside me. If I gave myself the time and quiet, I knew I would fall into thoughts as dreary as the winter weather itself.

The ride into town was once peaceful. When I was a young boy, I hadn't needed to worry about what went on in my father's mind. Neither of us knew at the time that such a rift would form between us. And within me. The child I had been loved the lighthouse and everything about it. Now, so many of my thoughts were occupied by wondering what life there was beyond my parents' expectations.

But it was never a good time to just leave, was it? Whenever I entertained the idea of moving away from the light, another of my elder siblings beat me to it. Or my mother took ill. Or the finances were in ruin and they needed my salary desperately. And before I knew it, I was nearing 30 years old with no plans to take me away from the life my father had written out for me.

Our wagon rolled over a bump in the road, jolting me out of my melancholy. I blinked. By then, we had made it far enough inland that I could no longer hear the distant crashing of ocean waves. My ears had grown accustomed to the sounds of the horses and their equipment. All there was now was the wind. It rustled through the branches around us, snapping off twigs and dropping them to the ground.

Once we emerged from the trees, the road wound around several small farms. A grin spread across my face. At this point in our trip, our distant neighbors would often walk over to chat with us. Most of the conversations were an exchange of news or asking if we could pick something up for them from town. Occasionally, someone would ask for a lift into Portland. And we would oblige. Not everyone had a large springboard wagon to head into town with, after all.

The smell of baking bread wafted into my nose and I knew we were about to pass my favorite farm. The Clinkman's.

Mrs. Clinkman had a natural talent for the art of baking. Her passion for confections was something of a local legend in those days. She or her husband would come out to the road if they saw us and offer my father and I a loaf of warm, fresh bread. We would always promise to share it with our family, but it often didn't survive the journey into town. Its scent overpowered our desire to share.

But today, the winter chill warded off all those who would have greeted us. So, the silence continued until my father finally decided to break it.

"I hope you will continue to work for the Lighthouse Service," he said. After the hours of silent travel, the sound of his voice seemed strange, almost foreign. "It has been my dream to hand down the running of the light to you when I retire."

"I know." I struggled to keep my voice steady. Whether it was anger that he would bring up such a sore subject or sadness at the reminder that time was passing quickly, I wasn't sure. But it didn't matter. Whichever emotion it was, I had to keep it under control.

I nodded, more to myself than to him, and said, "I will miss my life at home if I leave." But deep in my heart, I kept thinking of those ships passing me by and how much I wanted to be on one of them.

He huffed in response and I knew he wasn't satisfied with my answer. My heart ached. As much as I wanted to please him, I refused to set my happiness aside any longer. I deserved to live my own dream after serving his for so long.

We rode for a few more minutes, neither of us speaking. But I am almost certain that his mind raced just as much as mine. And yet, I couldn't guess at his exact thoughts. Was he devising ways to prevent my departure? Or was he asking himself where he went wrong with me?

I let myself drift in my thoughts for a while, trying to determine if perhaps my father was right. I was selfish for wanting to abandon my family. But the days at the lighthouse drew on longer with each moment that I wasn't exploring the seas. One hour could have been an entire season as far as I was concerned.

Could I live with myself if I stayed? And what would happen to Mother and Father if I left? Who would take care of the light? Would my brothers be able to take on that responsibility? I fidgeted with my hands, picking out dirt from beneath my fingernails.

When I became too uncomfortable with my thoughts, I decided to risk breaking the silence. "What do you think they'll do to prepare the house for the holidays?"

"I trust that whatever Carrie and the boys come up with, your mother will be pleased," Father said. He kept his eyes strictly focused on the road ahead. "You know how excited she gets about Christmas. And that's what matters."

His tone was sharp, as if he was pointing at me, accusing me of something. I cringed in spite of myself.

He slipped an old pipe out of his coat pocket and started to clean it. These days, he rarely smoked but he always kept it on hand. Just in case. His fingers worked at polishing the outside of the already spotless pipe with the hem of his jacket. If there was one thing I had inherited from him, it was the tendency to disguise feelings of discontent with work. And we were both known to the community as hard workers.

The edge of town raced towards us and, before I could even think to admonish him for his habit, we had arrived. I swung down from the wagon just outside of the Portland General Store.

"Be quick, Joseph," Father said.

"Will do," I mumbled, striding through the front door of the shop. The store consisted of a singular rectangular room with a door to the storage closet on the far end. The whole place was dimly lit by candles and packed to the gills with any goods a man could want. Except oranges. The fruit stand was the first place I checked. I bit back my disappointment and turned to greet the shopkeeper, Mr. Hendricks. In my haste, I hadn't noticed him sitting on a stool behind the front counter.

"Morning, Joe," he called, folding his newspaper with a distinct crinkle. "I set aside some chickens for your mother. Take a look, yeah?"

He lifted a series of small cages up off the floor and placed them on the counter beside his newspaper. I grinned at the plumpness of the eight chickens. Surely, he had selected the best birds available.

"Thank you, sir," I said.

I settled up with him and he had his clerk take the chickens to the wagon. When we were alone, he leaned conspiratorially toward me.

"You hear about Buffalo?"

"New York?"

"Where else?" In his excitement, his voice raised from a low murmur to a shout.

I jumped back to spare my ears. But I couldn't help the smile that stretched across my face. These were the chats that I looked forward to all week. Mr. Hendricks preferred to keep himself well informed on the goings-on of the world. His favorite topic was the future and any technological advancements. As such, he always sold the latest fashions and gadgets in his store.

"They're being electrified. And soon, the whole country will follow suit," he said, spreading his arms wide in a grand gesture. He threw his head back and laughed with gusto.

"That would sure be something."

Many of the country's newspapers covered how power was to someday be provided across the country. Apparently the first electric power plant had opened, and it was already regarded as a big success. There were now twelve lights along the waterfront in Buffalo with many more to follow.

"Technology has the power to change the world and, before you know it, it'll be unrecognizable. We had all better get used to it!" He winked as he weighed a package on his scale.

"Well, I don't know about that," I said with a light chuckle.

"What? That lighthouse of yours wouldn't benefit from being lit by electricity?"

"I suppose it might make less work for us." For some, that might be a blessing. But I couldn't say I was eager for it. After all, what would I do without the distraction of labor and watching over the fire? I waved my hand in dismissal. "Oil is too reliable to be replaced."

Mr. Hendricks's face flushed red. But before he could scold me, his wife, Cynthia, pushed her way through the door at the back of the room. She had a basket of extra scarves and gloves braced against her hip.

"Honey, are you bothering this young man?" she asked. Her eyebrows knit together in a playful glare. "Go get the canned goods labeled, would you?"

"Cynthia, dear…"

"Go on!" Mrs. Hendricks set her basket beside a near empty shelf and filled in the holes with her new items. "Joe, please give your father our regards."

Mr. Hendricks sulked into the storage closet. I held onto my laughter until I was able to exit the store.

Walking out onto Portland's main road, I bent over and was overcome by a fit of hysterics until I caught sight of my father leaning against our wagon with the sheriff, Benjamin True. True had occupied the position for over two years and had cultivated a reputation for being a dedicated member of the community.

He was a broad-shouldered man with the well-trimmed beard of a banker and a penchant for the finer things in life. There were rumors that he had his own live-in tailor to sew his suits. I had spoken to him only a few times so I couldn't say otherwise. But it seemed unlikely. He was a man of God, after all.

That day, he wore an indigo topcoat over a matching vest and crisp white shirt. He sported a thick leather belt and two holsters for his pistols – a 40-year-old Colt Dragoon and a brand-new Schofield. In a town as peaceful as Portland, it was unusual for a sheriff to be so heavily armed. I figured he just liked all the attention the revolvers earned him. As far as I had seen, he never used them.

My father noticed me and waved me over to them. I jogged the fifteen feet between us.

"Is there a problem?" I asked, crossing my arms as I settled in beside my father.

"Not for you," Sheriff True said with a smirk. "I was just telling your father about the cable I received from the harbormaster in Buenos Aires. I'm on the lookout for a ship."

"But that's so far!"

My father nudged me with his shoulder and fixed me with a deliberate stare. "Excuse my son, Sheriff. Please continue."

"As I was saying, *Annie C. Maguire* pulled out of the harbor without paying her docking fees. Her owners are in arrears and I have been asked to seize the ship when it makes port. I would be much obliged if you could keep your eyes open for it. Let me know if they happen by."

Sheriff True wore a placid expression as if he was talking about something as mundane as the weather. I wondered if he had seen worse than Portland's drunken sailors, not that they were that bad, mind you. Just a little rowdy and prone to get into fistfights over spilled ale. He had the serious disposition of a man who had served in wartime. The idea sent a cold chill rippling down my spine.

"Shall I invite both parties to tea?" my father replied.

True quirked an eyebrow and I made a show of checking in with our horses to hide my grin.

My father coughed. "I will keep an eye out."

"Good man," the sheriff said, patting his shoulder.

And with that, True pushed himself off of our wagon and marched toward the north end of town. The hem of his overcoat swayed in time with his stride. Then he disappeared down a side street. I turned to my father.

"Do you really think we'll see her?"

He shrugged. "It isn't a bet I'd place my money on."

Without another word, we got into the wagon to head back home. The sound of horse hooves striking the ground filled my ears uninterrupted until my father mumbled something under his breath.

He circled the wagon back to the harbor and pulled it up to Mathiew's Pub. George Mathiew had come to town nine years earlier and settled down to open a large pub near the docks. Father liked to stop there and chat with the owner and enjoy a pint. I liked listening to the men who came off the ships talk about their travels, and to learn what was going on in the world.

"Why the detour?" I asked. "Fancy a pint?"

My father shook his head with a deep laugh. "Detective work. And maybe a pint after."

I frowned but found myself nodding. If it had anything to do with the sheriff's request, I questioned whether the pub patrons would cooperate. But then again, some sailors shared gossip with abandon. Even the owner himself kept his ear to the ground about the ships, crews and cargo that came to Portland. He was certainly more agreeable than most.

George was a small fellow who was probably never clean-shaven in his life. He always had a smile and a bad joke to tell but most important to me, he shared my interest in far off places. As we entered, he was stationed behind the bar, cleaning glasses.

"Afternoon, George," Father said.

"Ah, Joshua! Good to see you." George set down the glass he had been working on and began wiping down the bar with an old rag. "What can I do for you?"

"I was wondering if you might have some information for me." He gave the other men nearby a cursory look. Then he leaned in, voice lowered. "Any news of *Annie C. Maguire*?"

"Might have heard some whisperings…"

My father dug in his pocket and pulled out a quarter. With little ceremony, he dropped it into George's outstretched palm.

"She's being pursued by creditors," he said. "The boys figure her owners are trying to make off with her and the load of cash in her safe."

"Interesting."

"It's all hearsay," George said with a shrug. Then he raised his voice, putting an end to that line of questioning. "How about an ale for you both?"

While my father responded enthusiastically, I was more subdued. I couldn't shake the eerie feeling that settled over me. Like I had become entangled in spiderwebs. I dusted off my arms.

A tall glass of ale clanked down in front of me. I flinched. "You all right there, Joe?" George asked, squinting as he examined my face. "Looking a tad pale."

Sweat beaded on my brow. It was hot, stifling almost. I didn't know how I hadn't noticed the heat from the roaring fireplace until that moment. My fingers fumbled with the buttons of my coat.

"I… Yes, I'm fine." Unbidden, my eyes slid across the open room.

It was so full of sailors that I could see almost no empty seats at the tables. I met the gaze of one that was seated nearby. A mountainous man with curly ginger hair and a beard that was just a few shades too dark. The eye contact sent chills throughout my entire being.

"I just need some air," I stuttered when I noticed my companions' concern hadn't waned.

Without waiting for a reply, I spun on my heel and retreated into the cold. A fresh breeze filled my lungs. I leaned against the pub's front wall for a moment, catching my breath.

The door creaked beside me. I looked up, expecting my father to be there. But it was the red-haired sailor. He lumbered passed me then stopped scarcely three feet away. I gulped.

"Afternoon," he said. "I couldn't help but overhear your conversation with the barkeep… And I thought to give you some advice."

"Thank you, but…"

He raised a bushy eyebrow and I let my protest die in my throat. "Listen, boy, I've been a sailor a long time now. I know trouble when I hear it. Sometimes, the love of a ship can run so deep; they would do anything to keep her. You aren't the law. Leave well enough alone."

Then he was gone. His warning hung in the air like a fog. I braced my hands against the wall behind me, knowing that even a subtle breeze could send my shaking form tumbling into the trampled snow.

Father stepped out of the pub soon after. By then, it was nearing 2 o'clock and I let my worry about household chores wash over me. Anything was better than hearing those words repeating in my mind.

"We should get on our way," I said, struggling to maintain an even tone. "I wouldn't want to miss the holiday dinner."

"Me neither," he agreed.

I expected him to ask about my episode, but he seemed unconcerned. Or if he was, he didn't want to upset me by mentioning it again. I hoped it was the latter.

The rest of our journey was spent in silence. About a half hour out of Portland, the weather started to turn for the worse and a light snow began to fall. I immediately buttoned my jacket up to ward off the cold.

"Keep an eye on the trail," Father said as he leapt down to the ground.

I took the reins to guide the wagon as he walked alongside the horses. He was worried about them stepping into a snow-covered hole. Many horses met their untimely ends on days like this. The only cure for a broken leg back then was to put the horse down. I owe it to Father's kind attention to our horses that I never had to see such a thing.

He remained mindful of the horses the entire journey home.

When we arrived at the house, Mother ran out to greet us. She helped us unload the wagon and examined the chickens. With a quick nod of approval, she set about preparing our Christmas Eve dinner with my brothers and sister in tow.

She glanced over her shoulder on the doorstep. I saw a tiny smile tug at the corners of her lips. "I am sorry you did not find your oranges!"

~ CHAPTER 4~

CHRISTMAS EVE

By the early evening, the rich smell of Mother's cooking drifted into my nose from the kitchen. My stomach growled in anticipation for dinner. I knew it would be delicious, even though I couldn't identify what she had made solely from its scent. Her food was always expertly put together and seasoned.

My brothers raced each other around the porch while they waited for dinner to be ready. Father worked hard to clean the oil house, occasionally peeking a head out to see if my mother had come out of the kitchen yet. I think he was keeping himself busy to avoid the temptation of stealing a taste of the meal.

My sister, Carrie, and I were in the parlor. It was our sacred tradition to lay out the holiday decorations. Each of us had a stocking to hang by the fireplace. When I struck out on my own, it would be my turn to take down my stocking and take it with me to wherever I settled.

In the days leading up to Christmas, Carrie filled her spare time by creating arrangements of dried leaves and paper crowns. She now spread these throughout the parlor. I scrubbed the floor clean beside her. By this time of year, it was coated with dried mud. Both of us were determined to do our part. With Mother putting so much effort into the cooking, the very least we could do was to make the family room presentable.

Carrie had developed my mother's disposition, a serene confidence. Life was an opportunity rather than a challenge. And there was no problem that could lead her from that stance. She was a girl who made the most of each day and reveled in the work. Not only had she spent weeks on the decorations, she also managed all her chores with ease.

Each Christmas, she would add more detail and planning to her handiwork. She strived to improve on anything she had to do more than once. This year, she was adding a paper Santa to each of our windows. Last year, she created wreaths of pine branches that she put on the doors to our house and the tower.

We often discussed our shared dream of living an adventurous life in a far-off land. Today, as she and I worked to decorate the parlor, I decided to tell her what I heard in town about *Annie C. Maguire*.

"And when I left the pub, a strange man followed me and warned me to mind my own business," I finished with a slight shudder. The image of him was still fresh in my mind and I imagined he might make an appearance in future nightmares.

Her eyes went wide as she listened. "How exciting!"

"You think so?"

"Of course." She looked at me and placed a paper crown on my head. Her voice slipped into that of an actor reciting drama. "Imagine this, oh captain, you are at the head of a mighty ship, stealing away in the night with a fugitive crew. Every port from Buenos Aires to Portland is hostile. And somewhere behind you, the law is following."

I scoffed in amusement. "I should think it isn't quite like that. The owner is just trying not to lose his ship because he couldn't make the payments in time."

Snowstorm at Portland Head Lighthouse*, created by Mark Robinson*

She rolled her eyes at me. "My idea is better."

"It always is," I said, allowing a grin to overtake my face. Then I shook my head and frowned. "Try not to get your hopes up, though. The odds of us seeing such a ship here are slim."

A few minutes later, Mother clanged the large bell that Father had hung on the porch. Dinner was ready.

Her timing was perfect. We had just finished with the parlor and, outside, the weather was becoming less pleasant by the second. What once had been a light snow with a slight breeze was now a proper storm. My brothers sprinted inside, shaking snow from their coats. Father was right behind them. Although I had been inside most of the day, I felt their relief at being able to leave the cold behind.

I glanced out the window, watching the snow fall densely on the ground. Tomorrow, we would have to shovel a path to the oil shed and the lighthouse if we were to keep things running. By the look of things, we needed to wake up earlier by at least an hour. We would experience severe delays otherwise.

Our brothers paid no mind to the decorations, but our father froze when he saw them. His gaze swept over the entire parlor, lingering on the leaf arrangements. Carrie pouted at our brothers.

"Even more beautiful than last year. Excellent work," Father said, dropping the extra firewood he had brought in. He leaned down to take off his boots and was nearly knocked over by Carrie's hug.

"I'm so happy you like it." Her gloomy expression had melted at his words of approval.

Father returned her hug then picked up the wood. He quickly built up a fire in the fireplace. The leftover wood was stored nearby. It would be used to keep the flames burning through the night. Maine was always cold in the winter and it wouldn't be Christmas Eve in our house if it did not feel like a hot day from summer. My mother always joked that, in our house, Christmas Eve was the warmest night of the year.

"You really outdid yourself," I agreed, gently guiding her to her seat at the kitchen table.

The boys were already sitting down in their respective spots and Mother set down plates of food in front of them. Despite their eagerness, they refrained from digging in. They knew that holiday dinners were much more formal than our usual ones. We each had to name one thing that we accomplished or learned that week. Only then could we enjoy our mother's cooking. It had been this way for as far back as I could remember.

"The lighthouse is starting to take shape with our labor, isn't it?" I asked as I sat down beside Carrie.

"Yes, it definitely is!" Mother replied. She finished doling out the food and took her seat at one end of the rectangular table. Father was across from her.

"Shall I go first?" I turned to Father and, when he nodded, I said, "This week, I helped Father finish the storage shed in the garden. I am really proud of how well it turned out."

"When you and your father work together, the results are always impressive," Mother said with a small smile.

"We should build a rope bridge across the rocks, don't you think? Maybe even a small dock," I added.

"Well, maybe during the summer, but not with this weather," Father replied as he laughed heartily.

My brothers talked about their schoolwork and chores with an exaggerated enthusiasm. The faster they got their words out, the sooner they would be able to eat. It was the biggest meal of the year, after all.

"I learned that the Clinkmans are a generous family," Mother said. She gestured to our plates. "They came all the way down here to gift us this goose."

Carrie discussed her improving knitting skills and our father, of course, told us about his meeting with the sheriff earlier that day.

"You all had best be on the lookout for the *Annie C. Maguire*," he said. His tone was flat but his eyes gleamed. Like he thought he was telling a clever joke.

After we had all spoken about our day, my mother gave her permission to begin eating. The smell of the food had nagged at us for too long. My brothers, who had been whispering excitedly to each other fell silent. It was an expectant silence as all the children waited for Father to take the first bite. The only thing we could hear was the crackling of the wood in our fireplace and the faint sound of snow landing on the ground.

He lifted his fork to his mouth then paused. "I hope you are all thankful for this feast. There are many people in the world who can only dream of what we have."

I caught my youngest brother's eye across the table. He hastily dropped his gaze to his plate. But not before I recognized the guilt. I wanted to reassure him. If I could, I would've told him it was all right to be excited to eat. Yet the words wouldn't form.

Father surveyed our reactions for a moment. With a quick nod, more to himself than anyone else, he began eating in earnest. The rest of the family didn't hesitate to follow his example.

"The bird is beautifully cooked, my love," he said once he swallowed.

Mother smiled. "Thank you."

"What happened to the chickens?" I asked.

"I thought I would serve them tomorrow," she replied. "The Clinkmans were just so excited for us to try their goose, I didn't have the heart to make them wait."

Father and I chuckled while my younger siblings smiled into their meals. We knew all too well how Mother liked to please everyone.

Dinner stretched on for several hours. Father began a conversation about how the area was growing so fast. Soon enough, steam ships would overtake the traditional sailing ships. I shared his opinion. The docks in Portland were now full of steam ships and coal bunkers to fuel them.

My mother brought up how we needed a new, larger oven to feed us all. She lamented the time it had taken to prepare the meat and pickled vegetables. But all the while, her lips smiled, and I knew she didn't mean it. Cooking was her favorite hobby – one that was definitely encouraged by the rest of the family.

My brothers and sister discussed taking a trip down to Boston in the new year. We all liked this idea except for my father, who fretted over the expense.

"Such a trip is an extravagance! Who would run the light while we are gone?"

"I am certain we could find someone…" Carrie's voice rang out like a small bell in the distance. But beyond the single sentence, she didn't protest further.

I was the last to speak up. "Someday, I would like to try my hand at being a sailor."

Father narrowed his eyes at me. Then he turned to face Mother. "Really, this meal is wonderful. You did such a great job."

She rested her hand on top of mine. In spite of her physical support, I knew she wanted me here to help Father with his work.

"I'm glad you think so," she said.

I was disappointed by the lack of response but did not want to cause an argument on Christmas Eve and decided to let it go.

By 9:00 pm, I had to dismiss myself from dinner to take my up post in the tower. Each night, someone had to be at the top to look out for ships and attend to the weights that kept the light spinning.

To be honest, I looked forward to the solitude. I would often bring a book with me to read in my spare time. Nothing ever happened during the night shift. It was a welcome respite from the noise of my family. The highlight of most evenings was watching the occasional ship, gliding by like a shadow. And if the snowfall worsened, I wasn't likely to see anything at all.

I hugged Mother and Father and gave each of my siblings a wave. Then I headed out into the night. Carrie ran out after me to hand over my scarf which I had left draped over a hook next to the door.

"Thank you for the help with the parlor." She stood on her tiptoes to peck my cheek.

"Anything for you, Carrie. Just make sure everyone stays indoors this evening to enjoy our handiwork," I responded, patting the top of her head.

She beamed brightly then raced back into the house. The night was now mine.

I kept a small lockbox up in the lantern room for the nights that I was up there alone. In it, I had a box of matches, a candle or two, my reading glasses and a book to pass the time. On this evening, I settled down to read *Life on the Mississippi* by Mark Twain. I saw him as someone who never let the water flow by him but rather wanted others to see him flow by.

I flipped the book open to where I had left it from my last night shift. Every few pages, I paused and walked around the light, gazing out into the ocean. When I saw a ship – a rarity on a night such as this – I tried to identify it. Then I would write down her name and the time she passed in a logbook that we kept in the lantern room.

At 11pm, Father joined me in the tower. I nearly jumped out of my boots when I noticed his presence. It was unlike him to change the shifts around. Unless someone was sick.
"Is something wrong?"

He shook his head with a mischievous smile. "I forgot to give you your Christmas gift… A long night's sleep!"

I blinked, not exactly seeing the humor in his statement. He coughed slightly.

"And this." He passed me a medium-sized package. It was relatively flat and done up with a white ribbon that was the clear handiwork of my mother.

I smiled back at him and took the present. Unwrapping it, I found myself holding a copy of Mark Twain's *Roughing It*.

"I thought you would want something to read after you finished your current one," Father said.

"Thank you." My cheeks grew hot and I was thankful for the cover of darkness. "I didn't get you anything…"

"You working with me is already a gift," he replied as he gave me a hug.

For a moment, I just stood in his arms. Hugs from my father were not common and this one caught me off guard. I almost didn't know how to react. But I wrapped my arms around him anyway. The affection he showed me that night has stuck with me ever since.

"I appreciate it." I released him then agreed to turn in for the evening. With a final glance, I left him to the tower.

Only 30 minutes later, as I was finishing washing up, I felt the floor tremble beneath me. The shrill screech of wood giving way filled my ears, chilled my blood. I stumbled down the stairs into the parlor just as Father burst through the front door.

His eyes were wild, voice unsteady as he yelled, "All hands turn out! There's a ship ashore in the dooryard!"

~ CHAPTER 5~

THE ANNIE C. MAGUIRE

Upstairs, the rest of the family crashed out of bed. I shoved my feet into my socks and shoes as Father sprinted back into the snow, leaving the door ajar. Only the frigid wind blowing into my face reminded me to take my jacket. I jogged after my father, heart pounding in my chest too hard for me to run faster.

Less than a hundred feet from us, three ship masts jutted up into the sky. Father stopped as if trying to assess the situation. My eyes were stuck on the scene before me and I ran right into him.

I was dumbfounded. "What is that?"

"Good Lord, boy! It's a ship!" he said.

And before I could recover my wits, he continued, "Grab the ropes and hooks from the storage shed. I will get one of the ladders." He didn't wait to see if his instructions were obeyed.

Far above me, the clouds blanketed the moon and the snow fell in thick sheets. But the yellow light cut through the darkness with ease.

How could this happen? If I could see it, so could the ship's crew. I shook the thoughts from my head. Thinking about anything other than rescuing the people aboard would do me no good now.

I reached the shed in seconds and threw open the door. Inside, I gathered up all of the ropes and grappling hooks I could fit in my arms. Then I took off again, struggling to keep a firm grasp on everything as I moved.

When I got to the end of the bluff, I could see the ship more clearly. It had grounded on the large rocks just a few dozen paces off the end of the bluff. Her hull groaned against the rocks as the waves crashed into her again and again.

Annie C Maguire crashed against the rocks beside the Portland Head Light, December 24, 1886, courtesy of the Maine Historical Society

On the deck, the crew frantically sprinted around the ship, trying to secure cables and barrels that had broken their straps. They moved with the rolling of the ship, as only an experienced crew could. Even the jarring movements couldn't throw them off balance.

"We have to get them off before she breaks up," Father said as he paused beside me. He carried the ladder on his shoulder.

There was a small land bridge between us and the rock where the ship was grounded. We climbed down the bluff so we could cross it. I remembered how, in the summertime, my brothers and I dashed over it to sit on the rock and fish. But now, it was slippery with the mixture of snow and seawater.

Father went first, doing his best to clear the slush with his boot. I followed. My experience with this bridge made me less cautious and my foot slid against the wet stone. I threw my arms out for balance. If I lost it, I would fall into the water below. Or worse, the jagged rocks.

A hand grabbed my shoulder, steadying me. I muttered a thank you to my father. The embarrassment made my legs shake but I focused harder on making it across. In those next few moments, I could barely breathe. My chest hurt from the lack of air when I finally set foot on the top of the rock.

I heaved a sigh of relief as I looked across the deck of the ship. Beside me, my father appeared perfectly composed.

The crew stopped as they noticed us. By then, the ship was listing heavily starboard and a few of the men were now struggling to stay upright. They had dropped the sails as well as the anchor in a last-ditch effort to keep her still. Any movement could break her up against the rocks.

We stepped up to the edge of our rock. There was a generous gap between us and their deck.

Father raised his voice to be heard above the wind and waves. "What ship is this? How many of you are aboard?"

An older man with cracked spectacles and a dark hat peered over the railing. "*Annie Maguire!*" He had a strong New Englanders accent. "And eighteen, including my wife and son."

"Is anyone injured?" I yelled.

"No. Only my pride!" the man said. I almost couldn't hear him over the wind's shrieking.

The rest of the crew approached the railing. They gathered around the older man and listened to orders I couldn't hear. He carried himself with confidence in spite of the severity of the accident. I knew from the way his crew hung on to his words that he was the captain.

I turned to Father. "Perhaps we can run a line and they can climb down." My throat was already sore from the effort of constant shouting.

He shook his head. "There is too much movement with the ship. Some of them might not be able to hold on. We are better off lashing the ladder to the side of the ship and letting them climb down that. As the boat leans towards the rocks, they should be able to step off the ladder easily enough."

I wasn't sure I agreed with his assessment. But with no other idea coming to mind, the only choice was to follow his orders.

"We will lift up our ladder," my father shouted to the captain. I recognized the strain in his voice. Any more pressure and it might fail him. "It is not long enough to reach the ground. I need you to lash it to the railing and have everyone climb down. As the ship rocks downward, they can step off and we will catch them!"

My father spoke with such certainty that I could not help but be impressed. The sentiment didn't stay with me. At each groan from the ship, my eyes were drawn to the pierced hull. If she broke, I had little doubt that we would be struck by the rubble.

The captain frowned and cast swift glances around him. Whatever he was looking for, he didn't find it. He turned his full attention to us. "It will be so! Pass it up!"

We hoisted the wooden ladder just high enough for the top rung to be within reach of the crew on the ship. Two of the crewmembers grunted as they reeled it in. Then it disappeared over the railing. Almost a minute passed but the ladder did not return.

Father's lips twitched into what I supposed was a smile. "Maybe they're stealing our ladder."

Before I could respond, they began to lower it over the side of the ship. This time, with several ropes attached to the top and the sides.

My father climbed higher up the rock to get a better view onto the ship. "They have secured it to the mast and the railing…it should hold!" He then slid down and waited with me.

"We are sending the first one over!" The captain's voice was distorted by the wind.

The first man over the side was a portly man with a white beard. His large peacoat caught on the railing until he ripped the fabric clear. As he worked his way down the ladder, we watched him struggle, helpless. He stopped on the bottom rung. By then, his face was streaked with sweat and seawater and his muscles threatened to give up on him.

He looked down at what was only three feet or so and gulped. "I can't do it!"

"You will do it or you can go back up to the deck and go down with the whole blasted thing!" Father said. "Jump and we will catch you. On the count of three, let go. One, two…"

But before he got to three, the man released his grip on the ladder. He landed on the two of us and we collapsed under his great weight.

I pushed him off of me and to the side just in time to hear the sound of wood splintering. I could not see where it was coming from, but it didn't matter. It was a warning. Our time was running out and, before long, the *Annie C. Maguire* would be nothing but a washed-up skeleton.

41

The clatter of wood hitting the rocks behind me startled me out of my thoughts. I whirled around in time to see Mother tying down our second ladder against the side of the bluff.

"Send them up as they make their way off the ship." Her voice was scarcely audible over the roaring waves.

My two brothers stood with her, ready to help in any way they could. I felt a pang of pride in my heart. That was my family. A brave father, a mother with all the answers, and siblings that supported each other through the worst.

Father yelled, "Send the next one down!"

He turned around to me and said more quietly, "I do not know how much time we have."

I looked over to the fellow who had just come down and realized that he must have been the ship's cook. Except for his coat, he was ill dressed for the weather and still had on a dirty apron.

I called to him, "Make your way up the ladder and there will be folks to help you across to the lighthouse."

He blinked heavy eyelids. Then, realizing that it was his turn to say something, he nodded and said, "Yessir."

He struck the first rung of the second ladder and started to haul himself up. At the top, my younger brothers waited with outstretched hands. They each grabbed an arm when he reached the final step and pulled him to safety.

A scream split the air. I spun around to see a large woman in a bright blue dress stepping onto the first rung of the ladder. She was wearing heeled boots and a wide-brimmed hat that matched her dress perfectly. If that wasn't odd enough, she clutched a hat box to her chest as she attempted to climb down the ladder.

"Drop the box! It's not worth your life!" My father's shout made her flinch.

But she held on to it like it was her newborn child and screamed back, "Never!"

My father's gaze shifted to me then back up to her, considering the situation.

"I will get her," I said.

Before he could try to stop me, I jumped on the ladder and climbed up to her. "Stay still. I'm here to help."

I brought myself up to her level, my hands grabbing the rungs beside hers. It was an awkward position. Pressed against her back, trying to wrestle the box from her.

"Give it to me and I will pass it down to my father," I said. "He will keep it safe for you. And it will be much easier to climb down without your hands full."
She shook her head no, a motion that loosened her grip on the ladder. As her fingers slipped, she screamed in terror. My ears rang long after her shriek had died out.

"Take it! Take it!"

With one hand firmly planted on the rung, I reached around to take the box. My wrist ached at the weight of it. I certainly hadn't been expecting an empty package to weigh so much.

"Drop it," my father said.

"It is very heavy!"

"I said, drop it!"

I obeyed. It fell into my father's arms with a thud. He set the hat box to the side. My companion on the ladder followed the movement with hawkish eyes.

I didn't have the time to think about what her concentration meant. "I will move my legs and arms down the ladder one step at a time. You need to follow me as I do so."

She clenched her teeth and nodded.

Slowly, I moved down a step and said, "Now you do it."

Every muscle in her body trembled as she followed me. But she did it. I resisted the urge to praise her. Something told me that she wouldn't take kindly to my approval. The last thing I needed was her snapping at me.

When I reached the bottom step, I dropped down to the stone where my father was waiting with a steadying hand. I told her to do so as well and that I would catch her.

"Let go on the count of three," I said, preparing myself to support her. "One, two, three! Three… Three…"

Before the fourth three, she released the ladder. My father and I caught her, saving her from falling to the rocks.

My father rested his hand on her arm and said, "Miss, we will help you up the ladder where my boys are waiting to take you safely inside."

She moved quickly to the ladder but paused when she started to step onto it. She glanced over her shoulder. "What about my hat box?"

"We will send that up too as soon as everyone is safely off the ship," my father said. His fingers wrapped tightly around her arm and he walked her to the second ladder. "Up you go, miss."

She crawled up the rungs as if it was the first time in her life. As she was doing so, the next person climbed over the rail of the ship and started scaling down the ladder. This time, it was a small boy, who could not be a day older than 12. He needed no direction from us; he slid down the ladder faster than I could have done.

He looked very pleased with himself and, glancing back up to the ship, he said, "Father said it would be harder than that. Where is Mother?"

"She went up the ladder," Father replied, gesturing vaguely behind us. He was too focused on helping the next person.

"Another one on the way!" he yelled.

Without another word, the boy stepped onto the ladder and started climbing up.

And so it went for the next half hour. The crew stepped onto the ladder one by one and made their way down. Every so often, one would stop out of fear or because the ship was moving too much to continue but eventually, all of the crew had escaped the wreck. They were quickly welcomed in to enjoy the hospitality of my mother, brothers and sister. All, save one.

The captain stuck his head over the railing. "I am passing down the logbook!"

He lowered a bundle down over the railing. It was wrapped in canvas and secured with a thick string. The captain had looped a line through this string and used it to lower the logbook. When it got down to us, my father took his knife and cut it loose.

"We got it!" My voice cracked from the strain.

And then it was the captain's turn to climb down the ladder. As he hoisted himself over the railing, a wind blew in, carrying with it what seemed like a wall of snow. My father braced the ladder and yelled up to the captain, "Hurry!"

The captain did not respond but the ship did. She whined against the rocks as her wood cracked in several more places.

He moved deliberately down the ladder stopping only to brace himself when the ship shuddered or when the wind picked up again.

When he landed with a loud exhale of pent up breath, my father grabbed him by his shoulder. "Is anyone else aboard?" I could barely make out his words over the wind. It had picked up strength, churning the snow around us.

"No," he said, standing a little taller.

My father pointed to the ladder going up the rocks and the captain, without hesitating, started climbing to my brothers.

"We will send someone into town tomorrow but for now, we need to make sure that everyone is all right," Father said as we watched the captain reach the top.

I nodded, too tired to get any words out, and motioned to my father to head up the ladder. Before I followed, I grabbed the hat box from where it sat on the stone. Then I scrambled up the ladder. I had only made it halfway when the hull shuddered and smashed down onto the rock. The ledge shook under the impact, nearly throwing me off the ladder.

I turned to watch for a moment. But the feeling of a splinter slashing across my cheek sent me up the rest of the way without a second thought.

My father then reached down to bring up the ladder. His voice competed to be heard above the now howling wind as he yelled, "Get inside and help Mother!"

My brothers and I climbed across the land bridge to the bluff and ran into the house with my father bringing up the rear.

~ CHAPTER 6~

CHRISTMAS DAY AT
PORTLAND HEAD LIGHTHOUSE

As my father headed to the shed to put away the ladder, I made my way to the house to help my mother. The snow fell hard around me. It clung to my jacket that was already soaked with the spray of ocean water. I shivered uncontrollably, eager to get into the heated parlor. The wind whipped around me and I realized that it was beginning to freeze my clothes.

I opened the door to the house and was immediately blasted by the warmth inside. My brothers crouched by the fireplace. I could barely see them through the crowd of guests. The boys finished stoking the fire to a blaze then squeezed through to the kitchen.

Carrie and our mother brought out plates of our holiday leftovers to serve the unfortunate visitors.

It was around two in the morning now. In just a few hours, the weather became so thick with snow that I could hold my hand mere inches from my face and not see my fingers. The clouds gathered tightly overhead. They blocked out the crisp winter sky and all the frigid stars.

Portland Head Lighthouse (South View), *created by Sarah Alu*

But in my home, it was bright and shining. All of our guests had looked up when I entered the house. Some were startled and others just wore blank expressions. Both were opposite reactions to the same ordeal. I wondered what it would have been like on that ship. Sinking and not knowing whether they would live or die. It made us all more grateful for the food and fire.

The longer I stood still, thinking, the more food I smelled. Our chickens! My mouth watered and, in spite of a slight jealousy, I found myself more focused on finding other ways to help these poor people.

"Anything I can do for you, Mother?" I asked as I followed her back into the kitchen.

"No, my dear," she said, wiping a bead of sweat from her brow. "Your brothers have taken care of the chickens and now I am cooking them."

She glanced up at me from her work and frowned. "I know the chickens were to be our meal for Christmas day, but we simply do not have enough food for eighteen new mouths without them."

"That's OK, Mother." I gestured through the doorway to the parlor. "I'm just relieved that everybody's safe and fed. I'll get the extra bedding and wood for the fire so our guests can sleep."

I headed off to the storage shed then returned with my arms full of blankets and wood. In the family room, I hung my jacket up on its hook to dry. Then I set about distributing the bedding to our guests.

Father had come in from the cold and was now sitting down at the dinner table, talking with the captain.

"We were heading for Portland Harbor," he explained. His voice sounded choked, as if he was fighting off tears. "It had been such a long run from Buenos Aires… We just lost sight of the lighthouse and… Well, you know what happened."

My father simply nodded along with the story, but I couldn't help the skepticism that crept up on me. I remembered looking up at the light during the rescue. The visibility was good enough. How could they have missed it?

"And *Annie Maguire* was such a good ship too." The captain sniffled then dabbed at his eyes with a dirty handkerchief. "Must've caught a cold…"

The name sounded familiar to me, but I wasn't sure if that was because the captain had mentioned it during the rescue. Then it hit me. This was the ship that Sheriff True had asked us to watch out for. I tried to catch my father's eye, but he was too involved with reassuring our visitor.

A minute or two later, Mother came out of the kitchen with a large tray of chicken pies. My brothers and sister followed her, carrying stewed vegetables, bread, cheeses and beer.

The food drew everyone's attention and without a word, they all came to crowd around the dining table.

My father took this opportunity to say a few words. "We are grateful, on this day, that all of you made it safely ashore. It is not the way most people celebrate Christmas, but we can celebrate that nobody was hurt. Later today, we will send for the Portland sheriff and get you all sorted out but for now, please accept our hospitality and my wife's good cooking!"

There was a half second of silence between the end of Father's speech and the guests resuming their talks. They shoveled food onto their plates, stacking pieces of bread and piling up the vegetables. Each of the crewmembers took more than I thought any man could stomach. But here they were, eating all of it. I knew I would have to act fast if I wanted a meal for myself.

My mother pulled me aside before I could grab a plate. "In a few hours, you will need to go into town and get more food."

"And find the sheriff," Father said.

"Will do." My stomach cramped and growled as I spoke. I rubbed it self-consciously. Even though I knew no one else could hear it over the noise of at least nine conversations.

As I shouldered my way through the packed family room, I stubbed my toe on a hat box. I recognized it immediately as the box that the captain's wife had been clinging to earlier. Why discard it now? I leaned down and picked it up. If it was valuable enough to risk her life for, then, surely, she would want it now.

It was much lighter than I remembered. I glanced around the room. Everyone was preoccupied with their food and companions. I didn't see the captain's wife among them.

Just then, an odd feeling overcame me. I frowned. Then, with another quick look to be sure no one was watching, I lifted the lid. It was empty.

I closed the box. As I did so, the captain's wife strolled out of the kitchen.

"Excuse me, miss," I said, closing the gap between us.

"Oh! You're the boy who helped me down." She had two pieces of chicken pie and a heaping serving of vegetables on her plate. "Thank you so much, young man."

I brushed off her praise. "Anyone in my position would have done the same."

"You're so humble," she said, smiling and blushing. "Your parents have done very well to raise you."

My stomach growled again before I could reply.

She giggled. "Please don't let me get in your way. Our hero needs to eat just as much as we do, after all." Her eyes dropped to the package in my arms. "Is that my hat box? Wherever did you find it?"

"On the floor over there."
"Well, I sincerely appreciate you keeping it safe. Would you mind setting it by the door for me? I wouldn't want to forget it on my way out." She winked.

Before I could respond, she slipped through the crowd and disappeared. I scrunched up my brow. That was one of the strangest conversations I'd had in a while. Even if shock was to blame, it gave me a bad feeling.

But the captain's wife had been so bright and gracious. I didn't want to accuse her of anything. She was a guest in my home and one that had just survived a terrible ordeal too. It would be rude to make accusations based on the weight of a hat box. And, as she'd said, my parents raised me better than that.

I set the package down by the front door then finally strode into the kitchen. I grabbed a plate, piled it up with bread, vegetables, and cheese. The remainder of the chicken was to be left for our visitors.

They needed it more than I did.

I found an open corner and sat down with my plate. Carrie was across the room with the captain's son. She handed him one of her toys, gave him a hug, then rushed over to me.

"Are they actually here? Or is it my imagination?" she asked with a small smirk.

"Funny," I said, rolling my eyes. Then I got serious. "I'm proud of you. This isn't something you've ever experienced, yet you seem to know exactly how to calm everyone down."

"I had a good example to follow." She glanced over her shoulder at Mother.

"Carrie!" The captain's son ran to her, toy in hand. "Come play with me!"

She waved to me as the boy pulled her back into the crowd. I laughed to myself and shook my head. Children really had a way of making misfortune more manageable.

I gobbled down my food then took a short rest upstairs. The need for more food could be satisfied in a few hours. It wouldn't do anyone any good if I was too exhausted to lead the wagon.

I rose with the sun at around 6:00 am. Mother greeted me with a list of supplies. By the shadows beneath her eyes, she hadn't slept at all. Everyone else had settled down. Most were asleep or nearly asleep. But my mother still worked, cleaning the used dishes and counting out how much we had to spend on the groceries.

"You should rest," I said as I hugged her. "You've done enough."

She only shook her head.

I tried not to think about how tired she looked as I threw on my still damp coat. Outside, the weather had finally calmed. The clouds opened to let some sun peek through and shine on the blankets of snow in the yard.

When the horses were hitched up, I took off to town with my mother's list. I knew that the general store would be closed at this hour. But the owners lived above it and would certainly open to help.

As I approached the town, I saw Sheriff True and several of his deputies hitching their wagons. He glanced up when he heard my horse's hooves thudding against the street. His hand raised in a brief wave.

"I heard from the Clinkmans that you have some company," he said as I pulled up alongside him. "We were just setting out to see if we can help."

"Everyone got off the ship safely," I said. I pulled my list out of my pocket and showed it to him. "Though they eat more than both of our horses."

He chuckled then turned to one of his deputies. "Get all the food you can carry and bring it to the lighthouse."

I handed the man my list of needed supplies.
"Now why don't we head over there? Get things taken care of," Sheriff True said to me.

I nodded hastily then turned my wagon around. The sheriff rode his horse alongside me. As we made our way back to the house, I recounted everything that had happened the night before. Well, as much of it as I could remember.

He whistled loudly and said, "That is quite a Christmas present!"

At half past 7:00 am, we arrived at the house. He swung down from his horse and approached the porch where my father waited. Sheriff True gave Father a hearty pat on the back. Then I turned away to take care of the horses and wagon.

The sheriff was still talking to my father when I finished. Instead of joining them, I decided to head inside. It was much warmer outside than it had been yesterday, but I much preferred the heat of the fireplace.

"Remember, we lost everything in the sea chest," the captain's wife hissed.

Her voice was so low I almost thought I had misheard her. She flinched when she noticed me. Then the expression was wiped away and replaced with a smile.

"I trust you had a successful trip into town?" she asked as her husband avoided my eyes.

"Yes, very."

"Wonderful!"

I didn't have time to reply. The sheriff had concluded his talk with my father and marched inside to take statements from the captain and his wife.

"Morning, sir, ma'am." Sheriff True nodded to each of them. "Would you mind if I asked you some questions?"

I lingered nearby, just close enough to hear. The captain's wife clutched a lace handkerchief as she cried through her story. Occasionally, she would wipe at her eyes with it. Even though there weren't many tears to dry.

When asked about the sea chest, I saw the captain and his wife share a pointed look. It was fast, so fast, I could've imagined it. He hesitated a moment too long.

"We left everything behind on the wreck. Soon, the ocean will take all our belongings. Not that she needs them." He laughed feebly.

"Very well," True said. "I'll have my deputies search the ship before that can happen. Don't you worry."

He let himself out then strolled over to examine the wreck. A wagon loaded with food and extra clothing pulled up to the house. I left the parlor to help the deputy distribute the supplies.

The Portland General Store had been very generous. They must have given us enough food to feed our guests for the rest of the week. And several of our neighbors had donated used clothes and toys to the captain's young son.

My father and I forgot our duties for an hour or two and sat on the porch gazing out over the grounds, the water and the lighthouse. Although the weather had cleared up considerably, the snow had not stopped falling since last evening. It shone brilliantly white on the light station.

For as exciting as the night had been, I was glad it was all over. The sight of this place, with snowflakes drifting down and its peaceful beauty, made me feel a swell of pride. This was my home; it always had been. But it was different now. I suppose I never noticed how tightly knit our community was until they pitched in without being asked. We all just wanted to help however we could.

"What will happen to her?" I asked, nodding to where the sheriff and his deputies worked at salvaging the valuables from the ship.

My father shrugged. "He was ordered to confiscate the ship to pay for the debts. But that can't happen. Even a slight breeze could break her now."

My brothers and my sister ran by me on the porch, eager to make snowmen and snow angels and have snowball fights.

"I suppose we'll just have to wait and see," he said with a heavy sigh. "They might find things to salvage or they might not."

I thought back to the captain's wife, her suspicious hat box, and odd behavior but didn't say anything. After all, I had no real proof that she had done anything wrong.

I allowed my thoughts to drift away from her. As Carrie whipped a snowball right by my face, I began to understand what my father saw in this place. And in the work that we did.

Sometimes, in a place like this, the adventure came to you. Excitement was not always something that needed to be sought out. It was to be enjoyed while it lasted, but the peace afterwards should be savored as well.

For the first time, as I leaned back in my chair, my mind felt at ease. My two options were no longer tearing me in completely different directions. In fact, they had almost merged into a single path. I smiled.

"We need to get back to work," Father said, rising from his chair.

"I'll meet you in a minute," I said. I wanted to stay just a bit longer. As long as he would let me.

~The End~

~ HISTORICAL NOTE~

PORTLAND HEAD LIGHTHOUSE
&
THE SINKING OF THE ANNIE C MAGUIRE

Both Portland Head Lighthouse and the sinking of the *Annie C Maguire* are straight out the pages of history.

In 1787, the Massachusetts legislature appropriated $750 to begin construction of a lighthouse at what is today known as Portland Head. By 1790, the United States Government took over the responsibility for all lighthouses in the United States and it provided an additional $1500 to fund the completion of the lighthouse.

Upon completion, the tower measured 72 feet from its base to the lantern deck and was illuminated by 16 whale oil lamps. It was first lit, with much local fanfare, on January 10th, 1791.

Construction of the first keeper's house had begun a year earlier in 1790. After that, Massachusetts Governor, John Hancock, signed a purchase order. This dwelling was later replaced by a larger one in 1816. Sadly, other than some vague descriptions, very little was retained about the original structure.

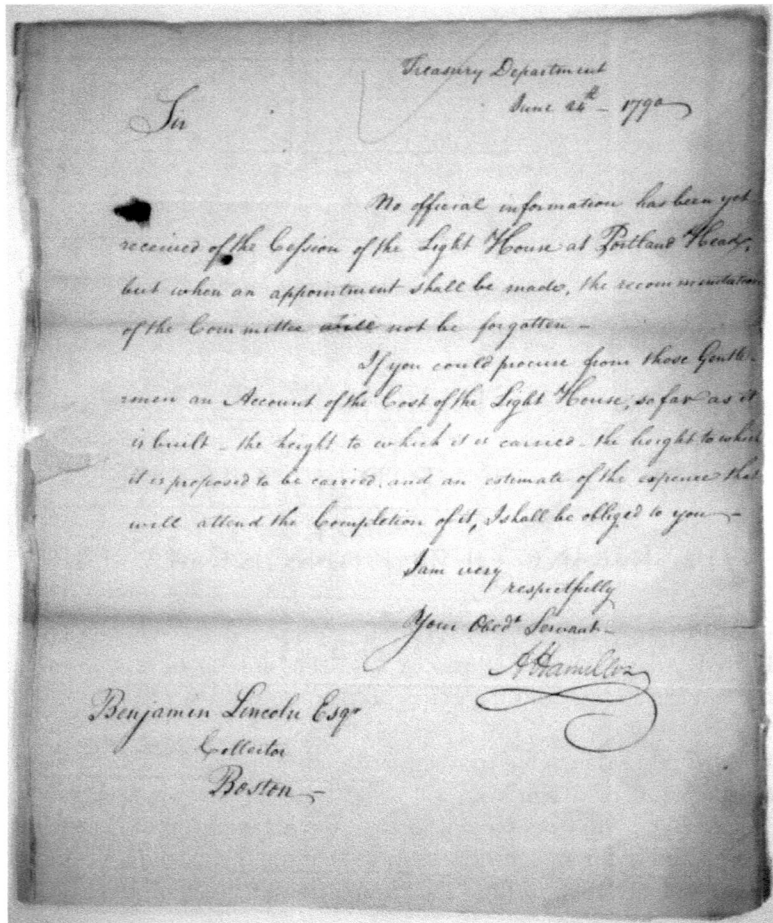

Alexander Hamilton's purchase order for the keeper's house, *courtesy of the National Archives*

By 1864, the lighthouse was scheduled to receive another upgrade. A 4th order Fresnel lens was added to the lantern room and a large cast iron staircase was added to the tower.

Less than a year later, the tower was raised another 20 feet and the lantern was upgraded to a 2nd order Fresnel lens.

***Anne C Maguire Shipwreck Monuments at Portland Head Lighthouse**,*
courtesy of quiggyt4 via Shutterstock

Late on Christmas Eve in 1886, *Annie C. Maguire* struck the rocks next to the Portland Head Lighthouse. There are several versions of both how the ship struck the rocks and how the crew was rescued. Joseph Strout claimed that the water was calm enough to permit the men "to jump ashore." Others have claimed the Strouts rescued everyone with a breeches buoy. But the most popular view is that the Strout family put a ladder across to the ship, and all aboard made it safely across the ladder to solid ground. Regardless, the Strouts were credited with saving the lives of the eighteen people aboard the ship.

Sheriff Benjamin True and his deputies made some effort to remove anything of value from the ship for the creditors but the ship itself was not salvageable.

The ship stayed afloat for about a week until the sea finally took her during a light storm on New Year's Day, 1887.

The hat box, the wife, and the sea captain play prominently into the history of the shipwreck as it was later discovered that they had emptied the contents of the ship's safe into it. It is unclear if Sheriff True was ever aware that the captain and his wife had made off with cash from the safe.

Joseph was the assistant keeper from 1877 to 1901 and later became the Head Keeper of Portland Head Lighthouse in 1904.

Portland Head Lighthouse & the USS Constitution,
courtesy of the Museum at Portland Head

Years after the shipwreck, Joseph Strout and his wife Mary had a son, John, who painted an inscription on the ledge where the *Annie C. Maguire* had wrecked to commemorate the event. Although it has been touched up with a fresh coat of paint to address the abuses of the weather and water now and then, it still stands today as a prominent warning to passing ships.

Four years after the sinking of the *Annie C Maguire*, the lighthouse received its last major upgrade. A new two-story keeper's house was built as a duplex for both the lighthouse keeper and the assistant lighthouse keeper and their families.

In the early 1900s, the land surrounding the lighthouse was developed as a coastal artillery site. Several artillery batteries were installed on the adjacent land on what is now known as Fort Williams Park. The many soldiers and their families stationed at the fort would have eliminated some of the natural isolation of the lighthouse.

Joseph retired from the United States Lighthouse Service in 1928. He lived out his remaining years in a small house near the coast in Rockport, Maine. His entire life was spent in the proximity of lighthouses.

During his years tending to the safety of others, he was a first-hand witness to the modernization of shipping. His life in the service would have started with shipping being predominantly driven by sail and then evolving into steam and ultimately diesel-based engines. Likewise, he would have seen ships evolve from wooden to steel hulls.

Today, Portland Head Lighthouse and the surrounding property are managed by the Town of Cape Elizabeth with the actual light and fog signal maintained by the United States Coast Guard.

The town has not only maintained the property but also established a museum and gift shop which is well worth a visit.

ABOUT THE AUTHOR

I am a finance guy-turned technology executive who moonlights as an amateur novelist/storyteller during the holidays. My work takes me all over the world, but I call Palo Alto, California home. Over the years, I have developed a passion for cycling, architecture, writing and cartography...all of which I've enjoyed in my career and my adventures with family and friends.

Every year, I create a series of short stories to keep my son entertained for the holidays. This year, I decided to publish one of them. This is actually my second book. My first book, Lean Business Planning came out in 2016 and was written to conduct entrepreneurs through the difficult and often trying thought process of starting a new endeavor.

Although I do not regard myself as a reincarnation of William Shakespeare, I enjoy the cathartic feeling of writing and have a fondness for sharing my personal stories and those that I have found on my travels. I hope that sentiment comes through in the pages of this book.

I also write, semi-frequently about business, travel and observations about life in my blog. You are welcome to read these accounts and learn more about me at www.markerobinson.com.

www.ingramcontent.com/pod-product-compliance
Lightning Source LLC
Chambersburg PA
CBHW071236170626
46809CB00008BA/3088